SPARKLE MAGIC!

By Kristen L. Depken · Illustrated by the Disney Storybook Art Team

A Random House PICTUREBACK® Book

Random House 🏠 New York

Copyright © 2015 Disney Enterprises, Inc. All rights reserved. Published in the
United States by Random House Children's Books, a division of Random House LLC,
1745 Broadway, New York, NY 10019, and in Canada by Random House of Canada Limited,
Toronto, Penguin Random House Companies, in conjunction with Disney Enterprises, Inc.
Pictureback, Random House, and the Random House colophon are registered trademarks of
Random House LLC.
randomhousekids.com
ISBN 978-0-7364-3366-2
MANUFACTURED IN CHINA
10 9 8 7 6 5 4 3 2 1
Glitter effects and production: Red Bird Publishing Ltd., U.K.

When Elsa was a little girl, she loved to use her sparkly snow magic to have fun with her sister, Anna. She made a snowman. She built snow mounds to slide on with magic that swirled and twirled.

Once, Anna got hurt. Elsa became afraid of her magical powers. She hid them away for many years.

But with Anna's help, Elsa learned how to control
her powers and use them for good.

Now Elsa is Queen of Arendelle, and there are
so many wonderful things she likes to do with her
sparkly snow magic! She helps old friends . . .

. . . and new ones!

Anna and Elsa have snowball fights
in the summer . . .

. . . and dress up in silly snow costumes.

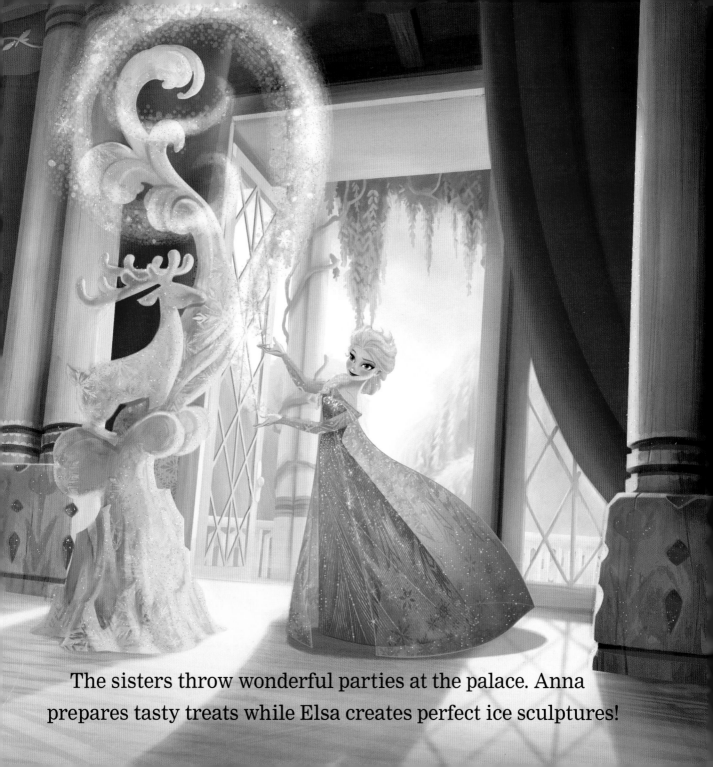

The sisters throw wonderful parties at the palace. Anna prepares tasty treats while Elsa creates perfect ice sculptures!

Elsa loves strolling through the kingdom
and playing with her friends.

She takes them sledding . . .

. . . and ice-skating!

Every day with Elsa is *snow* much fun!